MY DOG SPOT

WRITTEN AND ILLUSTRATED BY
Jack E. Levin AND **Norma R. Levin**

WITH A PREFACE BY THEIR SON
Mark R. Levin

Aladdin

New York   London   Toronto   Sydney   New Delhi

To our beloved family and loving families everywhere.

In memory of our precious Sporty, Prince, our three Ladys, and all cherished dogs.

For the happy and joyful times that should be every child's experience.

—Jack and Norma Levin

PREFACE BY MARK R. LEVIN

As you grow older, daily life seems to get a lot more complicated. It's important to remember that we are blessed, that life is good, and that there's much to which we should look forward. Still, if you're like me, in quiet moments you find a kind of happy refuge in the memory of your earliest youth, when times seemed much simpler and more innocent, and the news didn't matter all that much. I am fortunate to have parents who did their very best to ensure that my two brothers and I would be raised in a nurturing and loving environment, which we've strived to provide our own children.

When I think back to my earliest years, I recall so many wonderful moments. Even the little, routine, and trivial things bring a big smile to my face. I think about the many incredible people who've come and gone in my life, especially my grandparents and our precious dogs, including Prince and Lady (there would be a total of three named Lady over the years). I also remember fondly the friends and teachers who influenced my life, some with whom I've remained in touch and others whose whereabouts are unknown to me. But I know I speak for many who also find themselves traveling down memory lane from time to time.

My Dog Spot, conceived and developed by my parents, Jack and Norma, beautifully captures this sense of innocence and youth with the merry adventures of a dog named Spot. The purity of a simple story about a real dog—whose name was actually Sporty—illustrated with my father's folksy drawings, will no doubt rekindle your own childhood memories of your parents reading to you, as you read it and page through it with your own children. And I bet that one day, when your kids travel down memory lane, they will remember their wonderful youth too!

INTRODUCTION

Like *Proverbs for Young People*, *My Dog Spot* was almost sixty years in the making. Indeed, I found the original version in the same dusty old box stored in the same garage as *Proverbs for Young People*. But there are two significant differences. First, my darling wife, Norma, was and is my vital collaborator, as she has been throughout my life. Norma not only was an educator, having been an elementary school teacher and later proprietor (together with me) of Hawthorne Country Day School and Camp, she also has an exceptional ability to relate to young children through her caring and kindness. Second, *My Dog Spot* is about a real dog, whose actual name was Sporty.

I got to know Sporty the evening I first met my sweetheart and wife to be, Norma Rubin, at my sister's birthday party. I had offered to take Norma home after the party. It was there where Sporty, the Rubin family dog, greeted us at the door. Sporty was a fox terrier. He wasn't very large. He weighed about twenty to twenty-five pounds. Sporty was also full of life and energy. And as I soon learned, if Sporty knew you and liked you, he was sweet as sugar. If you were a stranger or he didn't like you, he could be tough as nails.

Sporty was quite a character! Norma would tell me about his different ventures and, as I came to know him, I witnessed them myself. Sporty was a beautiful little dog. We loved him and he loved us. But even then I was thinking Sporty would be the perfect subject of a children's book, so I suggested Norma keep notes of Sporty's antics. She did, which resulted in our book, *My Dog Spot*. The original unpublished version of the book was shared with the children who attended our nursery school decades ago. They loved it! And they loved Spot—our Sporty! Even now, sixty years later, we have very fond memories of this wonderful bundle of joy.

My Dog Spot is a happy story, with my fun illustrations that all young children will enjoy—and their parents and grandparents too!

Jack and Norma Levin
Boynton Beach, Florida

My dog Spot is white with black spots.

He has a
black circle
around his
left eye.

My dog Spot has pointed ears

and a long tail.

He is smaller than some dogs

and larger than others.

My dog Spot talks by barking, *Bow-wow.*

And laughs by yiping,
Yipe-yipe.

His tail goes up
when he's happy

and down when he's sad.

My dog Spot
can sit up and
beg for his
supper.

He likes to play with my daddy's slippers.

My dog Spot likes to

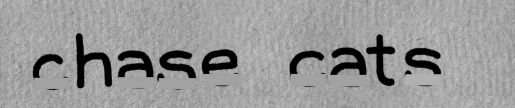

chase cats

and rabbits

and birds.

He likes to chew on bones

and then bury them
in the ground.

My dog Spot likes when
my daddy takes him

out for a stroll

He likes to put his head out the window when Daddy takes him for a ride in our car.

My dog Spot sleeps in his own little house,

and he has his own food and water bowls.

My dog Spot
loves me.

And I love
my dog Spot.

🪔 *Aladdin*

An imprint of Simon & Schuster Children's Publishing Division • 1230 Avenue of the Americas, New York, NY 10020 • First Aladdin hardcover edition May 2016 • Copyright © 2016 by Jack E. Levin and Norma Levin • Preface copyright © 2016 by Mark R. Levin • All rights reserved, including the right of reproduction in whole or in part in any form. • ALADDIN is a trademark of Simon & Schuster, Inc., and related logo is a registered trademark of Simon & Schuster, Inc. • For information about special discounts for bulk purchases, please contact Simon & Schuster Special Sales at 1-866-506-1949 or business@simonandschuster.com. • The Simon & Schuster Speakers Bureau can bring authors to your live event. For more information or to book an event contact the Simon & Schuster Speakers Bureau at 1-866-248-3049 or visit our website at www.simonspeakers.com. • Book designed by Laura Lyn DiSiena • The text of this book was hand-lettered. Manufactured in China 0316 SCP • 10 9 8 7 6 5 4 3 2 • Library of Congress Control Number 2015951619 • ISBN 978-1-4814-6907-4 (hc) • ISBN 978-1-4814-6908-1 (eBook)